The Adventures of MARY-KATE & ASHLEY™

THE CASE OF THE

U.S. SPACE CAMP®

VIOLET SWAMP IS WATCHING YOU

MISSION™

WILL SOLVE ANY CRIME • BY DINNER TIME™

DUALSTAR PUBLICATIONS PARACHUTE PRESS, INC.

DUALSTAR PUBLICATIONS PARACHUTE PRESS, INC.

Dualstar Publications
c/o 10100 Santa Monica Blvd.
Suite 2200
Los Angeles, CA 90067

Parachute Press, Inc.
156 Fifth Avenue
Suite 325
New York, NY 10010

Published by Scholastic Inc.

U.S. Space Camp is registered and owned by the U.S. Space and Rocket Center.

NASA name and logo used with permission of the National Aeronautics and
Space Administration at George C. Marshall Spaceflight Center.

With special thanks to Robert Thorne and Harold Weitzberg.

Printed in the U.S.A.
August 1996
ISBN: 0-590-88008-X
A B C D E F G H I J

Ready for Adventure?

It was the best of times. It was the worst of times. Actually it was bedtime when our great-grandmother would read us stories of mystery and suspense. It was then that we decided to be detectives.

The story you are about to read is one of the cases from the files of the Olsen and Olsen Mystery Agency. We call it *The Case of the U.S. Space Camp Mission*®.

Ashley and I couldn't wait to blast off for Space Camp. It was great! We zipped around in space suits, learned to walk on the moon, and steered a speeding space shuttle! And we still had time to track down the answer to a really *far-out* mystery!

The future of an entire space mission depended on us. You'll never believe how we cracked this case! Because no matter what, we always live up to our motto: Will solve any crime by dinner time!

Chapter 1

"Ashley!" I screamed. "Help!"

I held out a glass. Brown bubbles gushed out of the glass and poured over the table.

"Yikes!" Ashley yelled. "Your experiment is spilling all over our detective equipment!"

She grabbed our detective notebook off the table. And a pair of binoculars.

And a tape recorder and a magnifying glass. And our fingerprinting kit.

"Gross!" Ashley jumped back. "What is that stuff, anyway?"

"I was trying to make a space drink," I said. "I don't know why it bubbled up all over the place."

"That's no mystery," Ashley told me. "You're not a cook. You're a detective!"

I'm Mary-Kate Olsen. My twin sister, Ashley, and I are the Trenchcoat Twins. We solve crimes. We love mysteries.

But today we're excited about something else. We're going to Space Camp!

Space Camp is in Huntsville, Alabama, at the U.S. Space and Rocket Center. It's a *very* cool place.

Mom and Dad have a job at Space Camp. They are both computer experts. Space Camp wants them to write a new computer program for the space shuttle.

The good news is that we are going too.

"Forget the space drink," Ashley said. "We have packing to do! We leave for Space Camp tomorrow."

"I can't wait to be an astronaut," I said.

"We aren't going to be official campers," Ashley reminded me.

We'll be at Space Camp for only three days. Real Space Camp lasts for five days.

"But we'll still get to do great things. Mom

and Dad promised," she said.

"Too bad they didn't promise to let Trent and Lizzie stay home," I replied.

Trent is our big brother. He's eleven — and a real pain. He makes fun of us and is always saying that we aren't *real* detectives.

Lizzie is six. She thinks we're *great* detectives. She wants to be just like us.

"Lizzie won't bother us at Space Camp," Ashley said. "She's too little to go through astronaut training."

"True," I said. "But Trent will be there. And you know how he is."

"I know," Ashley said. She can't stand Trent's teasing either.

"But this time Trent is—" Ashley stopped talking as Trent burst into our office.

Clue was right behind him.

Clue is much more than a pet. She helps us solve important cases.

Her floppy brown-and-white ears hear things that we don't hear. Her big wet, nose sniffs out clues. She goes everywhere we go. She's even coming to Space Camp!

Clue wagged her tail. I patted her head.

"This time I'm what?" Trent asked Ashley.

"Uh, you're as excited as we are. About going to Space Camp," Ashley explained.

"Right," Trent agreed. "So get going. Mom says dinner will be ready in five minutes. And after that we have to finish packing." He turned to leave. And spotted the huge, brown puddle under our desk. "What's that mess?" he asked.

"A space drink that I made," I said.

"Are the astronauts supposed to drink it off the floor?" Trent hooted with laughter.

Clue sniffed at the spilled space drink.

"Go on, Clue" I said. "Have a taste!"

Clue licked at the bubbles. Then she whined as if she were feeling sick.

"Poor Clue!" Trent laughed.

I got a mop and began to clean up. "If you plan on staying up here, Trent," I said, "you've got to help mop."

"I'm going, I'm going." Trent headed for the stairs. "But do me a favor — don't serve that space drink at dinner!"

I groaned. "I'll never be able to have fun at Space Camp with Trent around!"

"Don't pay any attention to him, Mary-Kate," Ashley told me.

"You're right!" I said. "In fact, I won't talk to Trent at all!"

"Not at all?" Ashley asked. "But what if you need him to help you with something?"

"Trent? Help *me*?" I rolled my eyes in disgust. "That will never, ever happen."

"I guess," Ashley replied. "Anyway, you won't have time to worry about Trent. Starting tomorrow morning, we are going to be really busy — we'll be Space Camp trainees!"

Chapter 2

"This is so cool!" I exclaimed. "We're actually here at Space Camp. And the space shuttle is going to be launched any minute!"

"Not *any* minute," Trent corrected me. "In exactly *seven* minutes."

I glared at Trent. But I didn't say a word to him. Trent didn't notice. He was too amazed by Space Camp.

"It's huge," I said when I saw my first real rocket. It looked like a big, sleek airplane. And there it was, just sitting right in front of Space Camp.

"I can't believe that's the space shuttle."

Trent made a disgusted face at me. "That's not the real space shuttle," he said. "Anyone can see that."

"It looks real to me," Lizzie said.

"It does look real," Dad said. "But Trent is right. That's just a model. The real space shuttle is at the Kennedy Space Center, in Florida. Not here in Alabama."

"Right," Trent said. "How come you didn't know that, Mary-Kate?"

I still didn't answer him. I looked the other way.

Ashley nudged me. "Aren't you getting tired of *not* talking to Trent?" she whispered.

"Never!" I whispered back. I stared up at the space shuttle. "This might not be the real thing," I told Dad. "But it's still awesome!"

"It is," Dad agreed. "And wait until you get to fly in the Space Shuttle Simulator!"

"That's right," Mom said. "And here comes the man who will teach you how to do it."

Mom and Dad pointed across the lawn at a short man with black hair.

"Speedy is a counselor here at Space Camp," Dad said. "We met him last year at a conference on writing computer programs for NASA."

"What's NASA?" Lizzie asked.

"NASA is the short name for National Aeronautics and Space Administration," Trent answered. "N-A-S-A — get it?"

I turned to Lizzie. "Yes," I said, "and *I* know that NASA is in charge of all the United States' space missions."

Mom glanced at her watch. "Dad and I have to get to work, but Speedy will show you around."

"Hi, Jack! Hello, Terri! How are you doing?" Speedy greeted our parents. He quickly shook hands with me, Ashley, Trent, and Lizzie.

"Uh, hi, Speedy," I said. I had to say it fast. Because Speedy barely took a breath before he started talking again. He was the fastest talker I ever met. I could see how he got his name.

"It's really, really nice to meet you twins,"

Speedy went on. "But which of you is Ashley and which is Mary-Kate?" He squinted at Ashley and me. "I can't tell you apart. I don't know how you girls tell *yourselves* apart!"

"We may look alike," I said as fast as I could. "But we don't act alike!"

Ashley and I are both nine years old. We both have long strawberry blond hair and big blue eyes.

But Ashley takes her time about everything. She thinks and thinks about every problem. Then she thinks some more.

Not me. I work on hunches. I always want to jump right in.

"Ashley and I make a great team," I added. "Because we're *both* very good at solving mysteries!"

"Righty-o!" Speedy said — and went right on talking. "I can't wait to show you around. You'll see all the sights! You'll—"

"Sounds great, Speedy!" Dad interrupted. He was talking quickly too. "You kids have fun. See you later, all right?"

We all said good-bye and our parents hurried away. I think they were glad to get away from all Speedy's talking!

"Come on, gang. Follow me!" Speedy said. He took off running.

"Wait," I called. "Why are we running?"

"And *where* are we running to?" Ashley added.

Speedy looked back over his shoulder and smiled. "That's the big surprise!"

Chapter 3

"It's time for the *real* space shuttle to blast off!" Speedy called. "So follow me to Mission Control. We're just in time for the big countdown!"

We ran after him as fast as we could.

Right into Mission Control.

"Ten...nine...eight..."

"See? *That's* the real space shuttle." Trent pointed to a huge TV monitor that hung from the ceiling. On the monitor was a sleek white spaceship.

"That's the shuttle *Discovery*," Speedy said. "It's at the Kennedy Space Center in Florida, of course."

"Of course," Trent repeated.

"I knew that," I muttered.

I glanced around Mission Control. It was the most exciting place I had ever seen! Computers sat on long desks covered with important-looking switches and buttons. Colored lights blinked everywhere.

"Righty-o!" Speedy said. "Being at Space Camp is the next best thing to actually being at the Kennedy Space Center. We have a special telephone line that connects Space Camp's Mission Control with their Mission Control. We can see and hear everything that's happening when the *Discovery* is launched."

"Where is the *Discovery* going, anyway?" Lizzie wanted to know.

"Good question!" Speedy exclaimed. "*Discovery* is on a really special mission. It will carry a space probe into outer space!"

"What's a space probe?" Lizzie asked.

Trent groaned. "Little kids don't know anything!" he said.

Lizzie looked upset.

"Never ask Trent questions," I whispered to Lizzie. "All he does is make you feel dumb."

Lizzie turned to Speedy. "Speedy, can you tell me what a space probe is?"

"A space probe is a tiny explorer ship," Speedy said. "It can travel farther than the shuttle. And this space probe is heading all the way to Mars and Jupiter!"

"Wow!" Lizzie whispered.

"There are cameras inside the space probe," Speedy went on. "The cameras will take pictures of the planets. And the probe will send the pictures back to NASA."

Ashley turned to Speedy. "What happens if something goes wrong?"

"Wrong?" Speedy laughed. "Why would anything go wrong?"

The countdown continued.

"Four...three...two..."

"They're ready for liftoff!" Speedy clapped his hands in excitement.

Whoop-whoop-whoop!

Suddenly a siren sounded.

Clue leaped to her feet and barked.

Red warning lights flashed all around us.

"Uh-oh! Uh-oh!" Speedy shouted. He raced over to a computer screen.

Clue lay down and closed her eyes.

"What's happening?" I asked.

The countdown stopped. Then the siren shut off. The red lights went out. We all looked at Speedy.

"I don't believe it!" Speedy said. "Can you believe it? Everything was going so well. Then it happened!"

"What?" I demanded. "*What* happened?"

"The space shuttle isn't going anywhere," Speedy said. "The launch has been stopped!"

Speedy grabbed the special phone that let him talk directly to NASA. He spoke even faster than usual. He hung up and turned to us. He looked puzzled.

"NASA says their computer stopped the launch. And they don't know why. It's a mystery!"

A mystery? Here at Space Camp! Yes!

"Then it's a good thing we're here," I told Speedy. "Because Ashley and I are detectives. The Trenchcoat Twins!"

"You can't solve *this* mystery," Trent said. "This is the space shuttle we're talking about."

I ignored him. I whipped out my detective notebook and began to write: TIME: 10:27 a.m. WHAT HAPPENED: Space shuttle grounded. REASONS: ?

Just then Mom and Dad hurried into the room.

"Have you heard the news?" Dad asked. "Yes! The space shuttle couldn't take off," I answered. "And no one knows why. It's a mystery!"

Mom smiled. "Well, I wouldn't call it a mystery. It sounds like a computer problem."

"Right," Dad said. He brushed his thick red hair off his forehead. "We're flying down to Kennedy Space Center right away."

"And Lizzie and Trent are coming with us," Mom added.

"No way!" Trent cried. "Why can't I stay here at Space Camp?"

"We need you with us, Trent," Mom answered. "Lizzie's too young to be a camper. She has to come with us. But we'll be too busy working to look after her. Someone has to do it."

"And that someone is you," Dad added.

"Why can't Mary-Kate and Ashley do that?" Trent demanded.

"Sure! We wouldn't mind," I said. "I don't want to stay here. I want to be near the space shuttle computer. After all, there's a mystery to solve!"

"We're sorry, Mary-Kate," Dad said firmly. "We've made our plans. Lizzie and Trent will stay at the Kennedy Center. That's final."

Speedy turned to Mom and Dad. "I'll keep an eye on the girls for you," he promised. "And on Clue, too."

"Thanks, Speedy," Mom said.

Trent moaned. "No fair!" he said. "I want to stay, and I have to go. Mary-Kate and Ashley want to go, and they get to stay. It doesn't make sense!"

"I agree!" I blurted. "And I *never* agree with Trent! But it really *isn't* fair!"

"Or logical!" Ashley added.

Mom frowned at us. "Sorry," she said. "You and Ashley will have a perfectly good time right here. This shouldn't take long."

"But Mom," I said. "We want to help fix the shuttle!"

"You let us and NASA worry about the space shuttle," Mom said firmly.

"NASA is sending a plane to pick us up," Dad said. "It will be here in less than an hour. We'd better hurry."

Lizzie went with our parents to get ready. Trent hurried after them, arguing the whole time. He really wanted to talk them out of their plan. Good luck! Once Mom and Dad make a decision, they never change their minds.

Ring-ring! Ring-ring!

Speedy ran to answer the phone. He spoke into it — quickly, of course — and then raced to the fax machine.

"You girls *are* great detectives," Speedy

shouted.

"What do you mean?" I asked him.

"NASA said there *is* a mystery. A big one!" he said. "In fact, this is the *heaviest* mystery you'll ever have to solve! Because the space shuttle weighs over *4-million pounds* and has over one million parts. That means over one million clues and—"

Beep! Beep! Beep!

The lights on the fax machine started blinking.

Paper started rolling out.

"What's that?" I asked.

"It's a special emergency fax from NASA," Speedy told me. "And it's your first clue!"

Chapter 5

I hurried over to the fax machine. Ashley followed. Speedy grabbed the fax paper. He held it up for us to see.

Huh? Three black circles?

"That's the clue?" I asked. "It looks like a picture of three holes."

"Righty-o! These holes were found in the fuel tank," Speedy said.

"What's that?" I asked.

"Well, the shuttle has a tank for rocket fuel," he answered. "Just like a car has a gas tank. The fuel tank is attached to the space shuttle."

"I see." Ashley turned to me. "This means that it's *not* a computer problem."

"Right again," Speedy said. "NASA still

wants your parents to check out the computer system. But they *really* need to know where these holes came from."

"Would the holes keep the shuttle from flying?" I asked.

"Definitely," Speedy answered. "The shuttle can't take off until NASA is positive that it is absolutely safe."

I picked up my detective notebook. I quickly added our latest information. REASON SHUTTLE CAN'T LAUNCH: Holes in fuel tank.

"Ready to go!" Trent called. He poked his head into the room. "Mom, Dad, and Lizzie are waiting outside. Speedy, can you give us a ride to the Space Camp airport?"

"Sure thing," Speedy said. "Let's all go."

We followed Speedy outside and piled into his Jeep. Speedy drove — not *too* speedily — to the airport.

The NASA plane had just landed. We all climbed out of the Jeep.

Mom and Dad turned to say good-bye. They gave me and Ashley a hug and kisses. They gave Clue a pat on the head.

Ashley and I watched as Mom and Dad followed Trent and Lizzie. They all hurried up the steps and onto the plane.

"Hey, look — what's that?" I asked. I pointed at the back of the airplane.

Two men were unloading an enormous box. The box was bigger than Speedy's Jeep!

The two men loaded the big box onto a trailer cart. They drove away toward Mission Control.

"There it goes!" Speedy exclaimed. "Do you know what's in that box?" He gave us a wide smile.

"Your second big clue!"

Chapter 6

"A clue?" I looked at Speedy in surprise.

"Sure. Didn't I mention that NASA was sending a clue on the plane?" Speedy asked.

"No," Ashley said. "That's the one thing you *didn't* say."

Mom and Dad's plane took off for Kennedy Space Center. We waved good-bye until we couldn't see it anymore.

"Time to check out that clue," Speedy shouted. We drove back to Mission Control in record time.

The big box was in the center of the control room. Beside it stood one of the men who had taken the box off the plane. He was tall and had curly red hair. A bunch of shiny keys hung from the belt of his blue flightsuit. He carried a blue Space Camp flight bag.

Speedy rushed up to him. "Hiya, Flash!" he said. "Girls, meet Flash. He's a Space Camp counselor, just like me."

"Well, maybe not *just* like Speedy," Flash said. Flash spoke very slowly. He took a step toward us.

Jingk-jingk-jingk. His keys jingled loudly.

He placed his flight bag under a table in a corner.

"Flash! Guess what?" Speedy yelled. "Mary-Kate and Ashley are detectives. They're going to help me solve the mystery of the holes in the fuel tank!"

"Oh, right," Flash said. "Detectives." He gave us that look. The one grown-ups give us when they don't believe we're really detectives. "I'll be at my desk if you need me," Flash called. He walked down the hall.

Jingk-jingk-jingk.

"Flash doesn't act like he cares much

28

about the fuel tank mystery," I said.

"Oh, he does," Speedy told us. "Flash loves the space program. When he was younger, he wanted to be a space shuttle pilot. But he grew too much. He's one inch taller than an astronaut is allowed to be."

"He must be really disappointed," I said.

Speedy shrugged. He reached inside the box and pulled out an orange board.

It was big and full of holes.

"Wow! Is that the fuel tank?" I asked.

"Righty-o! Well, it's a *piece* of the fuel tank," Speedy said. "I helped make the very first fuel tank. That's why NASA sent it to me. They thought I could help figure out what put the holes there."

Speedy went to his desk and turned on his computer. "I need to check my records. I'll be right here if you need me," he added.

"But Speedy," I said. "Don't you want to examine the evidence?"

"That's the first thing a detective does,"

Ashley told him.

"Nope. Too busy. Can't talk now," he said.

I shrugged. "Well, time for us to get to work," I told Ashley. "Ready, Detective Olsen?"

Ashley grinned. "Ready, Detective Olsen."

I knocked on the fuel tank. "Feels kind of soft. Almost like wood," I said.

I checked out the holes with my magnifying glass. "It looks like these holes were punched into the cover," I told Ashley.

"I agree." Ashley measured them with her measuring tape. "And all the holes are about the same size," she added.

I pulled out my trusty detective manual. Great-grandma Olive sent each of us a copy when we decided to be detectives. The manuals told almost everything you needed to know to be a good detective.

"Let's see…" I flipped a few pages. "Here it is." I read out loud. "*Holes as clues: Here are pictures of things that make holes.*' Check out the golf ball." I held the picture next to a hole in the fuel tank. "The golf ball is smaller than the hole in the fuel tank. The softball is too big," Ashley said.

I held a picture of a meatball next to the fuel tank hole. "It fits!" I said.

Ashley groaned. "*Meatballs* made the holes in the fuel tank?" She shook her head. "I don't think so!"

"Then we're stuck," I said.

"What does our detective manual say about being stuck?" Ashley asked.

I quickly flipped through the pages. "When stuck, get more information. And pay attention to details."

"Hold on. Hold on, everyone!" Speedy called. "Look at the TV screens! Something's coming in from NASA right now."

The TV screen overhead showed the astronauts sitting inside the shuttle. They were still waiting for permission to lift off.

Speedy turned some dials. Suddenly we

could hear the astronauts talking and laughing. And we could hear a low sound:

Tap-tap-tap! Tap-tap-tap-tap!

"Doesn't that tapping sound bother them?" I asked. "It would drive me crazy."

"I guess they're used to it," Ashley replied.

Ring-ring! Ring-ring!

Speedy picked up the phone. He listened closely. "Oh, no!" he said. He hung up.

"What's wrong now?" I asked.

Speedy looked worried. "*More* bad news!" he told us.

Chapter 7

"NASA just found *more* holes in the fuel tank!" Speedy said. "We've got to find out where the holes are coming from—and *fast*. Because the shuttle absolutely, positively *must* be launched tonight!"

Jingk-jingk-jingk.

Flash walked into the control room.

"I heard the news. More holes!" Flash shook his head. "Maybe the shuttle will *never* be launched," he said.

Speedy chuckled. "Ha, ha! This guy's a real comedian. Of course it will be launched!" Speedy turned to Ashley and me. "Do you have any ideas yet?"

"Uh, not yet," I answered. I couldn't tell him our only idea so far — that the holes were made by meatballs!

"Forget about the holes. You'll never save this mission. Anyway, we have to go to a meeting, Speedy. It's time," Flash said.

Speedy checked his watch. "So it is. Well, girls, NASA and Space Camp are counting on you. Give it your best shot."

Speedy hurried out the door. "Let's go, Flash."

"I'm right behind you," Flash said. "Oh, I almost forgot. I left my flight bag in here." He turned to search the room. "There it is, under the table." He picked up his bag. Then he turned to Ashley and me.

"If I were you, I'd give up trying to figure out what made those holes," Flash told us.

I stared at him in surprise. "Why would we do that?" I asked.

"You're kids. Let the experts take care of the problem. You go on and have some fun—that's what Space Camp is for!"

Flash waved and walked out the door.

"Aren't we having fun?" I asked Ashley.

"Big time!" she answered. "What could be more fun than trying to solve a mystery? But we're already stumped. We don't know what made those holes."

"I have an idea," I said. "Instead of trying to figure out *what* made the holes, let's try to figure out *who* made the holes. Someone who *doesn't* want the *Discovery* to be launched."

"Remember how Flash acted when the mission was stopped? He wasn't upset, like Speedy was," Ashley remarked. "And we know that Flash couldn't be an astronaut."

"So let's put those facts together," I said. "Maybe Flash doesn't want anybody else to go up in the shuttle, either. Maybe he stopped the mission."

Ashley looked doubtful. "We can't prove that. Not without lots more information."

"You're right." I thought hard. "Where can we find more information?"

"There's a museum here at Space Camp," Ashley told me. "Museums are full of information."

I jumped to my feet. "Come on, Clue," I called. "Let's go check it out!"

We raced over to the museum. It was huge! I didn't know where to look first.

"Since we don't know what we're looking for, let's check out this room!" I said. It has space games. I'm playing first."

I practiced steering a spaceship through space. Of course, I was really watching a video screen. It showed asteroids and planets whizzing by.

Ashley tugged my arm. "Come on, Mary-Kate! We're running out of time!"

Ashley pulled me into the next room.

She turned and whistled for Clue. "Here, girl!" she called. "Come, Clue!"

Clue didn't come. She raced over to a display case. She jumped up at the case.

"Not now, Clue," I yelled. "We have to go!"

Woof! Woof! Clue didn't move.

Ashley and I hurried over. There was a big rock in the display case. Not just any rock — a moon rock.

"Come on, girl," Ashley said. "Let's go! Leave the rock alone!"

Somebody behind us chuckled. "I like that rock too. In fact, I remember the day we picked it up off the moon!"

I whirled around and saw an ordinary-looking man. I stared at him. "You picked up this rock off the moon?"

"That's impossible," Ashley said. "Unless you're an astronaut. Are you?" she asked.

"You guessed it," the man said.

"Wow! Then you must be Neil Armstrong!" Ashley shouted in excitement. "He was the first man to walk on the moon!"

The man smiled. "Not exactly," he said.

"Well, are you John Glenn?" I asked. "He's a famous astronaut too. He was the first American to orbit the earth."

"Not him either." The man chuckled again. "But I was the *fourth* man on the moon! I'm Astronaut Alan Bean. Of the Apollo Twelve space crew."

I stared at him in awe. "This is so exciting!" I reached out my hand. "I'm Mary-Kate Olsen," I said. We shook hands.

"And I'm Ashley Olsen," Ashley said.

"You're the Trenchcoat Twins!" Mr. Bean shook Ashley's hand. "You're famous too."

"But we never walked on the moon!" Ashley said. "Was it amazing?"

"You bet! A real out-of-this-world experience," Mr. Bean joked. "Though you don't actually walk on the moon—you bounce!"

"Why do you bounce?" Ashley asked.

"Because there isn't as much gravity on the moon as there is on the earth," Mr. Bean explained. "Gravity makes you feel heavy. When you're walking on the moon, you're *not* heavy. You're very, very light."

"Would I bounce on the moon too?" I

asked.

"Sure," he replied. "How much do you weigh on the earth?"

"About fifty pounds," I said.

"Well, on the moon you'd weigh only eight pounds," Mr. Bean told her. "That's nothing! Imagine how high you could jump!"

"It sounds awesome," I said.

"Actually I was scared sometimes," Mr. Bean replied. "After all, I was 240,000 miles from home!"

"I'm scared right now," I told him. "I'm scared we'll never solve our big space mystery. You're an astronaut. Do *you* know what might have poked holes in the shuttle's fuel tank?"

Mr. Bean frowned. "I don't know," he said. "But my advice is to keep an open mind. And never be afraid to ask for help. Sometimes you need all the help you can get. That's why astronauts always work in teams."

We thanked Mr. Bean and hurried away from the museum.

"We just met a real astronaut," I said to Ashley. "And he gave us great advice. But I'm not sure how to use it."

"Me either," Ashley said. She let out a big sigh. "If only we were at the Kennedy Space Center."

"But we aren't there," I said. "Face it, Ashley. We're stuck. This is one case we'll never crack."

"You don't mean—" Ashley began.

"Yes." I nodded sadly. "I'm afraid that Olsen and Olsen are through!"

We're Mary-Kate and Ashley—the Trenchcoat Twins! And we're going to U.S. Space Camp to solve a really far-out mystery!

There are strange holes in the U.S. Space Shuttle— and we have to find out how they got there!

Flash and Speedy, our new friends at Space Camp, explained that the Space Shuttle couldn't blast off until the mystery was solved.

No problem! The Trenchcoat Twins were on the case! We searched for clues in the Space Camp Museum.

**And we met Alan Bean there—a real live astronaut!
He gave us some out-of-this-world advice. He said
it's really important to keep an open mind.**

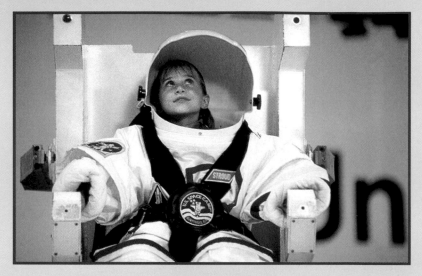

We put our mystery on hold to have some fun at Space Camp...

...and we found out that it's really hard to move in a spacesuit!

Space Camp training was a total blast!

5...4...3...2...1...Liftoff! We steered a make-believe space shuttle through a perfect pretend space flight.

"Shh! Listen," I suddenly said. "This shuttle doesn't make a tapping sound like the real shuttle!"

"Right," Ashley said. "*That* tapping sound came from outside."

Our dog, Clue, seemed to agree. She led us outside—to our best clue yet!

"Hey, look!" I said. "Up in the tree—there's the answer to the mystery!" Finally Ashley and I cracked the case. Can you?

Chapter 8

"Unless…" Ashley said.

"Unless what?" I asked.

"Unless we listen to Mr. Bean!" Ashley's eyes shined with excitement. "We need information from the Kennedy Space Center, right?"

"Right," I said. "And we can't go there."

"True," Ashley agreed. "But we could get help — from someone who *is* there."

I stared at her. "You can't mean Trent!"

"Keep an open mind, Mary-Kate," Ashley said. "That's what Mr. Bean said. And he said astronauts work in teams. So maybe Trent will be on our team."

Hmmmm.

"Do you think he would do it?" I asked.

"I don't know," Ashley said.

"Okay. I'll keep an open mind." I took a deep breath. "Let's ask Trent for help."

Clue followed us back to Mission Control. She lay down beside Speedy's desk. I reached for the phone and dialed the number Mom left us. Trent answered.

"Hi, Trent. How are you? It's me, Mary-Kate." I spoke as quickly as Speedy! "I guess you heard about those holes in the space shuttle. No one knows what made them."

"Ashley and I have a few clues," I went on. "But we need more information. Fast! So we were wondering if maybe you'd kind of help us out."

Ashley took the phone from me. "Trent, we need you to go to the NASA library," she said. "Read the records of the last shuttle launches. See if anything unusual happened."

There was a long pause. "Yeah...okay," Trent finally said. "It won't take too long.

And it'll be a lot more fun than playing with Lizzie."

I grabbed the phone. "Thanks, Trent. Thanks a lot," I said. Then I hung up and jumped up and down in excitement. When I jumped, a metal pipe rolled right under my feet.

"Where did that come from?"

Ashley came over to get a closer look. "I think it rolled out from under the table."

"I'll leave it on Speedy's desk," I told Ashley. I carried the pipe past the orange board from the fuel tank. "Hey, I have a hunch!"

I held up the pipe to one of the holes. The pipe slipped right inside!

"It fits!" I said.

"So what?" Ashley frowned.

"So, now we can say the holes were made by this pipe instead of a meatball!"

"Uh, Mary-Kate — aren't you forgetting something?" Ashley asked. "The holes were made at the Kennedy Space Center. In Florida. If this pipe made those holes, how did it end up here in Alabama? Did it fly here from Florida?"

Oops.

Ashley started giggling. Then she stopped. "Wait a minute," she said. "Maybe that pipe *did* fly here. Flash put his flight bag under that table, remember? Maybe the pipe fell out of his bag."

"So?" I asked.

"So Flash flew here with that bag. He flew here from Florida. That means Flash *might* have used this pipe to poke the holes in the fuel tank."

"We know that NASA wouldn't let Flash be an astronaut. And he told Speedy that we couldn't save the mission," I added.

"And he told us to drop the case," Ashley said. "Maybe he didn't want us to find out that he's guilty!"

"Then Flash is our number-one suspect," I

said. "Now all we have to do is prove that he made the holes."

"We'd better be careful," Ashley added. If Flash is mad enough to ruin a whole shuttle flight—"

"Just think how mad he'll be at us for finding out!" I shivered.

Suddenly we heard a noise in the hallway.

"What's that?" Ashley asked.

"I don't know," I answered.

The noise stopped.

Then we heard it again. Clearer this time.

Jingk-jingk-jingk.

"It's Flash!" Ashley shouted. "And he's coming this way!"

Chapter 9

I dropped the pipe. It hit the floor with a loud *clang* and rolled into the corner.

Jingk-jingk-jingk. The door to Mission Control began to open.

"Quick! Let's hide!" I whispered.

Ashley and I scrambled under Speedy's desk. We crouched down beside Clue.

Flash entered the room. He was searching for something. He spotted the metal pipe in the corner. He bent and picked it up. He left the room.

We popped out from under the desk.

"Flash *was* looking for the metal pipe!" I said. "He must be guilty!"

Just then the phone rang. I answered it. It was Trent!

"Guess what?" Trent asked. "Guess what happened at the last space shuttle launch?" He paused. "A fire broke out!"

"A fire?" I said. Ashley put her ear next to the phone so she could hear too.

"The rocket engines burst into flames on the launchpad," Trent explained. "But they put out the fire pretty quickly. Only a few nearby trees were burned."

"Anything else?" Ashley asked.

"Let me think," Trent said. "Well," he continued. "The report also said that there were some owls nesting in the trees. But the owls flew away after the fire. And they didn't come back."

"That's all you found out?" I said. "Thanks for nothing, Trent."

"Hey, I did my best," Trent said.

"Thanks anyway, Trent," Ashley told him. "Talk to you later."

I hung up the phone. "I don't see how a fire and a bunch of owls has much to do with this shuttle launch," I said.

"Remember," Ashley told me. "Pay attention to *every* piece of information."

I opened my detective notebook and wrote: CLUE: On last launch, shuttle rockets caused fire in nearby trees. Owls flew away.

"Hey! We forgot all about Flash!" Ashley exclaimed.

"Right! Let's try to find him," I shouted. "Maybe we can still pick up his trail!"

We raced into the hall. We stood still and listened. The building was quiet.

We hurried outside.

"Look, Ashley!" I shouted. "There goes Flash!"

Chapter 10

Flash headed toward a large building with glass doors. He pushed through the doors—and disappeared inside.

"Come on!" Ashley said.

We raced up to the building. We pushed open the door and walked into a huge, open room. It was full of Space Camp trainees!

"They must be doing their astronaut training!" Ashley explained.

We gaped at the shiny metal machines that sat all around the room. Each machine was surrounded by a group of kids. They all wore Space Camp uniforms and helmets.

"This is totally cool!" I said. "I wish I could be an official Space Camp trainee. Don't you, Ashley?"

"Yes," Ashley agreed. "But right now we have to find Flash. Where did he go?"

"He's got to be here somewhere," I said.

"Hey-hey-hey!" said a familiar voice. "Hold it right there!"

Speedy!

"So how do you like the Training Center?" he asked. "Pretty neat, huh?"

"Yeah, it's great, but—" I began.

"Glad you think so," Speedy said. "Because it's time for your special training session!"

"That would be terrific, Speedy," I said. "But we've got to chase Flash. Because he—"

"No way!" Speedy said. "Flash is busy. He just brought back some parts from the Kennedy Space Center. He has to fix a training machine that broke."

"But Speedy, we—" I began.

"No buts," Speedy replied. "I promised your mom and dad that you'd be instant Space Camp graduates. So now's the time to start your training! You're first, Ashley."

Speedy pulled Ashley over to a chair that was attached to a big metal frame.

He slipped a helmet onto her head. Then he fastened a seat belt around her waist. He strapped another belt around her shoulders.

"Wait!" Ashley yelled. "We have to find—"

Speedy didn't listen. "You're all set!"

"But Speedy," she said. "We really do need to go and—"

"Oh, so you want to move?" Speedy smiled. "Go on, Ashley. Move!"

Speedy gave Ashley's chair a push.

"Whoa!" Suddenly her head was down and her feet were up.

"Uh-oh, Speedy! I think this thing is broken!" she yelled.

"No, that's how the Five Degrees of Freedom machine works," he said. "It teaches you that it's hard to control the way you move in space—because you're almost weightless! Isn't it great?"

"No!" Ashley said. "Get me out of here, Mary-Kate," she called.

"Mary-Kate is busy," Speedy told her. "She's going to try the Multi-Axis Trainer."

Before I could run, Speedy strapped me into a very strange machine. This one had a chair that sat inside three big metal circles.

"Keep your hands on the handles," Speedy said.

"Wait, Speedy," I said. "What does the Multi-Axis Trainer do?"

"It lets you feel what it's like if your spacecraft is out of control," Speedy answered.

Out of control? Yikes!

Chapter 11

"Ready?" Speedy asked.

I didn't have time to say no. I turned head over heels and spun around in a circle.

"Eeeeeaaaaahh!" I screamed.

"Isn't it a great feeling?" Speedy asked. "There's no up or down in space. You can sleep or eat lunch standing on your head. And it's really easy to turn cartwheels!"

"I like it!" I told Speedy. "Once you get used to it — it's fun!"

Speedy helped Ashley out of the Five Degrees of Freedom machine.

"Time to try the 1/6 Microgravity Chair," Speedy called. "This one is high-flying fun!"

Speedy strapped Ashley into a chair that was fastened onto a tall metal pole.

"But Speedy, we really have to find Flash," Ashley said. She tried to wriggle out of the chair and bounced high into the air!

"*Now* what's happening?" Ashley yelled.

"This machine teaches you how to walk on the moon." He chuckled. "I mean *bounce* on the moon," he added.

"I know! I know!" Ashley said. "Because you're almost weightless on the moon!"

Meanwhile my chair stopped spinning. "Speedy," I called. "I still need to tell you something important about Flash."

"Well, tell me after you put on your space suit," Speedy said. "I happen to have two suits just your size! Come on!"

Speedy helped Ashley out of the 1/6 Microgravity Chair. He helped me out of my machine. Then he tossed two puffy white space suits our way. We put them on.

"Wow!" I said. "This suit is really heavy!"

Speedy laughed. "Righty-o! Working in the suit takes practice," he told us. "Especially when you have to build a space station."

I gasped in excitement. "Is that what we're going to do next?"

"You bet!" Speedy handed us each a metal ball. We were supposed to twist the ball onto the end of a long metal rod.

It was hard work! The space suits were so puffy that we had to move our arms really slowly and carefully. And our gloves made it extra hard to move our fingers.

"Got it!" Ashley cried. She tugged on the metal rod. The round ball fell off.

"Oops!" Ashley said. "Let me try again!"

"No time for do-overs!" Speedy said. "It's your turn for one last training area."

"That sounds great," I told him. "But we're forgetting one thing. Flash! We think he made the holes in the fuel tank."

Speedy shook his head. "That's crazy!"

"We found a metal pipe at Mission Control," I explained. "It fits into the holes on the fuel tank. And Flash brought that pipe back from Kennedy Space Center."

"And we think that Flash is angry because NASA won't let him be a space shuttle pilot," Ashley added.

"But Flash loves NASA," Speedy told us. "Even if he can't be an astronaut. He would never harm the space shuttle!"

Speedy checked his watch again. "You can ask him yourself. But later. Because right now it's launch time!"

Speedy ran into a training model of the space shuttle. "Come on!" he said. "You're going to fly into space!"

Ashley and I wriggled out of our space suits in record time.

We hurried into the model of the space shuttle cockpit. It was a very small room, filled with buttons and switches.

A long instrument panel took up the whole room. Three computer monitors were lined up in the panel side by side.

We pulled on our headsets. Speedy sat

outside and spoke to us over them.

"Okay," I said. "What do we do first?"

"Strap yourselves in," Speedy told us. "And prepare for liftoff!"

Yes! Ashley and I slapped a high five.

"Shuttle ready for countdown!" I called.

"Roger that," said Speedy. "T-minus 10 seconds and counting."

"Nine...eight...seven...six...five...four... three...two...one!"

Suddenly the cockpit started to shake. We could hear the roar of the shuttle's rockets.

It felt as if we were really blasting off!

We steered the shuttle through a perfect pretend space flight! When it was over, Speedy helped us out of the cockpit.

"Wasn't that a blast?" he asked.

"It was great, Speedy," I answered. "I wish we could stay at Space Camp forever!"

"Or long enough to finish the real five-day training program," Ashley added.

"Well, I can give you a special Space

Camp invitation to come back another time," Speedy said.

"Fantastic!" I shouted.

"I'll do it right now," Speedy told us. "Raise your right hands."

Ashley and I raised our hands.

"Do you, Mary-Kate and Ashley," Speedy began, "solemnly swear to strive to be the best that you can be and remember forever that what you learned here is for the betterment of humankind in the known and unknown universe?"

"Yes!" Ashley and I both shouted.

Speedy hung gold medals around our necks. "We usually give these medals to our outstanding trainees when they finish the program. But you can have yours now. If you promise to come back soon!"

"I promise," I said.

"Space Camp is incredible!"

"Especially the shuttle launch," I said. "It was like being on the real space shuttle."

"Yeah," Ashley agreed. "Except for the tapping sound."

Speedy looked at Ashley. "Tapping? What tapping? I didn't hear any tapping in the model shuttle."

"I know. Neither did I," Ashley said. "But the real space shuttle had lots of tapping."

Speedy scratched his head. "No, there's no tapping on the real shuttle. Tapping is not a space shuttle sound. No, not a tap to be heard—"

"But Speedy," I interrupted. "We heard the tapping sound today—when we watched the astronauts on the TV monitors."

"Maybe it was another sound—a hum, maybe?" Speedy asked.

"No. You're making a big mistake, Speedy," I said. "We definitely heard tapping."

Speedy frowned. "But if there's not supposed to be any tapping—" he began.

"Then there's only one possible explanation!" I cried.

Chapter 12

"That means the tapping is an important clue!" Ashley said.

"That's right!" I agreed. "Come on — we'd better check those video monitors!"

We all raced back to Mission Control. Ashley and I could barely keep up with Speedy.

We burst into the control room.

Woof! Woof!

"Hi, Clue!" Ashley said. "Good girl." She bent down to scratch behind Clue's ears.

Speedy turned on the TV monitors. One monitor showed the space shuttle on the launchpad. The other showed the astronauts, still waiting in the cabin of the shuttle.

Speedy turned a dial. Suddenly we could

hear the astronauts talking.

"No tapping," Speedy said. "Does any-body hear a tapping sound?"

Tap-tap-tap! Tap-tap-tap-tap!

"There it is!" Ashley cried.

Speedy turned down the sound on the cabin monitor. We couldn't hear the astro-nauts. But we could still hear the tapping.

"The tapping isn't coming from inside the space shuttle," I said. "It's coming from out-side — on the launchpad!"

"The holes are on the outside of the shut-tle," Ashley said. "And the tapping sound is outside the shuttle. So what's the connec-tion?"

Woof! Woof! Clue leaped up and rushed to the door.

"Not now, girl," I said. "We're busy. We can't take you for a walk."

Clue jumped up at the door. She whined. She raised her head and howled. Loudly.

"Okay, okay!" I told her. "But just a quick

walk. Because I have a hunch that we're just about to solve this mystery!"

Ashley and I raced outside with Clue. She ran toward the woods, then ran back to us.

Woof! Woof! She barked. Then she took off.

"Clue! Come back, girl!" I called. "This is no time to go exploring!"

Clue didn't listen. She ran farther into the woods.

We chased after her. But for once Clue was faster than we were.

We searched the woods up ahead. There was no sign of her.

"Where did she go?" Ashley asked.

"I don't know," I answered. "I can't see her anywhere!"

Clue was gone!

Chapter 13

Tap-tap-tap! Tap-tap! Tap-tap-tap-tap!

Ashley's eyes widened. "Mary-Kate! That's the tapping sound we heard outside the space shuttle!" she cried.

"You're right! What's it doing here?"

I ran toward the tapping sound—and found Clue. She wagged her tail and leaped up at a tree.

"Hey, the tapping sound is coming from this tree," I said. "It's so noisy! What do you think is making that sound?"

Ashley pointed into the branches. "It's a bird! A little bird with a long beak."

"What kind of bird makes all that noise?" I asked.

Ashley and I looked at each other. "A

woodpecker!" we shouted at the same time.

We both burst out laughing.

"Nice try, Clue," I told her. "But I don't think the tapping sound on the launchpad came from a woodpecker."

"Wait, Mary-Kate." Ashley frowned. "Remember — keep an open mind. And pay attention to details."

"I guess one of us has to take a look at that woodpecker's hole," I said. "And I guess that someone is me."

I climbed up the tree. I reached the place where we spotted the woodpecker.

The woodpecker had flown away. But it was easy to find the hole it made.

"How big is the hole?" Ashley called.

"Meatball size!" I called back. "Ashley, this hole looks just like the ones in the fuel tank!"

I scrambled down the tree.

"Are there woodpeckers in Florida?" I asked.

Ashley groaned. "I don't know. Now we need to find out about woodpeckers!"

I whipped out my detective manual. "There's nothing about birds in here," I said.

"I know," Ashley said. "Let's try the Space Camp library."

"Good idea!" I checked my watch. "But we'd better hurry. It's almost dinner time!"

Ashley, Clue, and I ran to the library. We found a big book on woodpeckers.

I quickly turned the pages. "Hey, look at this!" I said. "I found a big picture of an owl."

"That's strange," Ashley said. "Mary-Kate, check your notebook."

I whipped out my detective's notebook. "What am I looking for?" I asked her.

"That part about the owls," she told me.

I read through my notes. "Here it is," I said. I read out loud: CLUE: On last launch, shuttle rockets caused fire in nearby trees. Owls flew away.

"I still don't get the connection," I said.

Ashley leaned over the woodpecker book. "Well, maybe this will help," she said.

She read the words under the picture. "'Owls are natural enemies of woodpeckers.'"

"So? What does that mean?" I asked.

"Owls keep woodpeckers away," Ashley answered. "But when there are no owls around, there are plenty of woodpeckers."

"I get it!" I said. "The shuttle fire burned the trees and made the owls leave their nests. Then woodpeckers came to live there."

"Righty-o," Ashley replied.

I felt a burst of excitement. "Ashley, I think we just solved the mystery!"

Chapter 14

"Woodpeckers like to peck holes in all kinds of things," I told Ashley. "Tree limbs, and houses, and—"

"And fuel tanks!" Ashley shouted.

Yes! Ashley and I slapped a high five.

"Let's go back to Mission Control and tell Speedy!" I said. "He's not going to believe this!"

"Woodpeckers?" Speedy laughed. "First it's Flash with a metal pipe! And now little birds with big beaks?"

"But listen to this," I said.

I read through the notes in my detective notebook. I explained to Speedy about the fire during the last space shuttle launch.

"The fire burned some trees near the

launch pad," I added. "The owls that lived there flew away. And when the owls left, a whole bunch of woodpeckers flew in. And they made the holes in the fuel tank!"

Speedy listened carefully. "You girls make a lot of sense," he finally told us. "In fact, I think you solved this case. I'm going to call NASA right now!"

Speedy called NASA and told them everything.

"NASA will use their outside camera to check the launchpad for woodpeckers," he told us.

We all watched the TV monitors.

We saw the space shuttle on the launchpad. The camera pointed at a small dark spot on the fuel tank.

It zoomed in for a closer look.

A woodpecker!

And the woodpecker was definitely pecking a hole! Tiny orange bits of fuel tank flew everywhere.

The camera pulled back. We could see the whole space shuttle now. But we couldn't see the woodpecker.

"No wonder nobody noticed the woodpeckers," I said. "The fuel tank is so big. And woodpeckers are so small."

"Congratulations!" Speedy said. "Looks like you super-duper snoopers have solved another case!"

"Thanks to Great-grandma Olive," I said.

"And Alan Bean," Ashley added.

"And don't forget — Trent helped too," I said.

"Yes, they all helped," Speedy agreed. "But you and Ashley are still the best detectives I ever met!"

He gave each of us a high five. Then he shook hands with Clue, too!

"Can the shuttle blast off now, Speedy?" Ashley asked.

"Yes, now that NASA knows the astronauts aren't in danger," Speedy said. "They're going to scare away the woodpeckers. And make some quick repairs on the holes. Then the shuttle will launch, and the space probe will be on its way to Mars and Jupiter. The mission is saved!"

Ashley and I cheered. Clue barked.

"Oh!" Speedy said. "In all the excitement, I almost forgot. NASA said your parents will fly back tonight—after the shuttle launch."

Flash burst into the room. "NASA said you solved the mystery. Good work!"

"Thanks, Flash," I told him.

Speedy winked at me and Ashley. "I told you Flash had nothing to do with it."

"I came to help you fix this piece of the fuel tank," Flash told Speedy. "Then I'll fly the panel back to Florida. I can fix the rest of the holes right there."

"Good plan," Speedy said. "And the best part is that I get to stay here with Mary-Kate and Ashley. While you fly to Florida, we can take one more spin on the Multi-Axis Trainer and the 1/6 Microgravity Chair!"

"Cool!" Ashley and I both cheered.

A few hours later we were back in Mission Control. It was almost time for the shuttle launch. NASA gave the go signal. We watched the countdown on the TV monitors.

"Five…four…three…two…one…Liftoff!"

It was a perfect launch. The space shuttle soared into the sky.

"You did it, girls. You absolutely did it!" Speedy said. "And just in time, too!"

"Well, we always live up to our motto—"

"I know, I know," Speedy interrupted. "Will solve any crime by dinner time!"

"Or in this case—" Ashley looked at me.

"Launch time!" we said together.

That night our whole family was together again at Space Camp.

"I guess there was a mystery after all!" Mom said. "And you solved it."

Speedy pulled us all into the control

room. "NASA has a special thanks for the space detectives," he said. "Take a look at the TV monitors."

One monitor showed the outside of the space shuttle—it was in orbit in outer space! In the background was the blue-and-white Earth. It was beautiful.

The other monitor showed the inside of the space shuttle cabin. The astronauts were looking right at us!

The astronauts waved. "Hello, Mary-Kate! Hello, Ashley!" they called.

"We just wanted to say thanks from all of us up here," one of the astronauts said.

"If it weren't for you, we wouldn't be here!" the other one added.

"No problem!" I said into Speedy's microphone.

Ashley reached for the microphone. "Right," she agreed. "This whole case was out of this world!"

Hi from both of us!

Whew! Flying the Space Shuttle Simulator, whirling in the 1/6 Microgravity Chair, and meeting a real life astronaut who landed on the moon before we were even born—totally awesome! Solving the mystery of the NASA space shuttle was our most thrilling case yet!

But an even *more* amazing case was about to fly our way. Someone was trying to steal a very important airplane—an airplane that was going to deliver Christmas presents to kids all around the world! It was up to us to find the thief—before Christmas Eve! Could we crack this case in time? Find out in *The Case Of The Christmas Caper*.

And here's more big news. We are having the best sleepover party ever, and you're invited to read all about it in *You're Invited to Mary-Kate & Ashley's Sleepover Party*!

In the meantime, if you have any questions, you can write to us at:

MARY-KATE + ASHLEY'S FUN CLUB™
859 HOLLYWOOD WAY, SUITE 412
BURBANK, CA 91505

We would love to hear from you!

*love
Mary-Kate and Ashley*

The Adventures of
MARY-KATE & ASHLEY™

LIFTOFF WITH THE TRENCHCOAT TWINS™ U.S. SPACE CAMP® SWEEPSTAKES

YOU CAN WIN A PARENT/CHILD WEEKEND AT U.S. SPACE CAMP®, SEE A NASA SHUTTLE LAUNCH*, AND MEET THE OLSEN TWINS.

Complete this entry form and send to:
Liftoff With the Trenchcoat Twins
C/O Scholastic Trade Marketing Dept.
P.O. Box 7500
Jefferson City, MO 65102-7500

Name_____
(please print)

Address_____

City_____ State_____ Zip_____

Phone Number (_____) _____

DUALSTAR
PUBLICATIONS

*subject to availability
No purchase necessary to enter. Sweepstakes entries must
be received by 10/15/96.

SWEEPSTAKES RULES

OFFICIAL RULES:

1. No purchase necessary.

2. To enter, complete this official entry form or hand print your name, address, and telephone number on a 3" x 5" card and mail to: Liftoff With the Trenchcoat Twins™, C/O Scholastic Trade Marketing Dept., P.O. Box 7500, Jefferson City, MO 65102-7500. Enter as often as you wish, but each entry must be mailed separately and received by October 15, 1996 for a late Fall 1996 visit to the U.S. Space Camp and Rocket Center. One entry per envelope. Partially completed entries or mechanically reproduced entries will not be accepted. Sponsors assume no responsibility for lost, misdirected, damaged, stolen, postage-due, illegible or late entries. All entries become the property of the sponsor and will not be returned. Odds of winning depend on number of eligible entries received.

3. Sweepstakes open to residents of the United States, children no older than 14 as of October 30, 1996, except employees of Dualstar Entertainment Group, Inc., WarnerVision Inc., Parachute Press, Inc., Scholastic Inc., U.S. Space and Rocket Center, their affiliates, subsidiaries, respective advertising, promotion, and fulfillment agencies, and the immediate families of each. Sweepstakes is void where prohibited by law.

4. Winners will be randomly drawn on or about October 30, 1996, by Scholastic Inc. whose decisions are final. Except where prohibited, by accepting prize, winner consents to the use of his/her name and photograph or likeness by sponsors for publicity purposes without further compensation. Winner will be notified by mail and will be required to sign and return an affidavit of eligibility and liability release within 14 days of notification attempt, or the prize will be forfeited and awarded to an alternate winner.

5. Grand Prize: A three (3) day, two (2) night trip for a parent and child (2) to a weekend session at the U.S. Space and Rocket Center (date of trip to be determined by sponsor by 10/30/96) to see a shuttle launch and meet the Olsen twins. Shuttle launch subject to availability. Not responsible for changes in NASA flight schedules, inclement weather or other delays/cancellations. Children must be between the ages of 7 and 14 to attend.If winner is unable to attend on specified date, winner can select an alternate date, without the Olsen twins' visit or the shuttle launch. Includes round-trip coach air transportation from airport nearest winner's home to the U.S. Space and Rocket Center, three (3) nights U.S. Space Camp lodging and meals. (Est. retail value $2,500). Grand prize winners must utilize prize within twelve (12) months subject to flight accommodations availability.

6. Prizes are non-transferable, not returnable, and cannot be sold or redeemed for cash. No substitutions allowed. Taxes on prizes are the responsibility of the winner. All federal, state, local laws apply. By accepting prizes, winners agree that Dualstar Entertainment Group, Inc., WarnerVision Inc., Parachute Press, Inc., Scholastic Inc., U.S. Space and Rocket Center, and their respective officers, directors, agents and employees will have no liability or responsibility for any injuries, losses or damages of any kind resulting from the acceptance, possession or use of any prize and they will be held harmless against any claims of liability arising directly or indirectly from the prizes awarded.

7. For a complete set of rules, or winners list, send a self-addressed stamped envelope by December 30, 1996 to: Liftoff With the Trenchcoat Twins™, C/O Scholastic Trade Marketing Dept., P.O. Box 7500, Jefferson City, MO 65102-7500.

It doesn't matter if you live around the corner...
or around the world...
If you are a fan of Mary-Kate and Ashley Olsen,
you should be a member of

MARY-KATE + ASHLEY'S FUN CLUB™

Here's what you get:
Our Funzine™
An autographed color photo
Two black & white individual photos
A full size color poster
An official **Fun Club**™ membership card
A **Fun Club**™ school folder
Two special **Fun Club**™ surprises
A holiday card
Fun Club™ collectibles catalog
Plus a **Fun Club**™ box to keep everything in

To join Mary-Kate + Ashley's Fun Club™, fill out the form
below and send it along with

U.S. Residents – $17.00
Canadian Residents – $22 U.S. Funds
International Residents – $27 U.S. Funds

MARY-KATE + ASHLEY'S FUN CLUB™
859 HOLLYWOOD WAY, SUITE 275
BURBANK, CA 91505

NAME:_____

ADDRESS:_____

CITY:_____ STATE:_____ ZIP:_____

PHONE: (____) _____ BIRTHDATE:_____

~The Adventures of~
MARY-KATE & ASHLEY ™
THE VIDEOS

Look for these best-selling detective home video episodes! Starring the Trenchcoat Twins™, your favorite stars, Mary-Kate & Ashley Olsen!

And also available:

Distributed by KidVision, a division of WarnerVision Entertainment. All rights reserved.
A Warner Music Group Company.
TM & © 1996 Dualstar Entertainment Group, Inc.

High-Falootin' Fun
for the Whole Family!

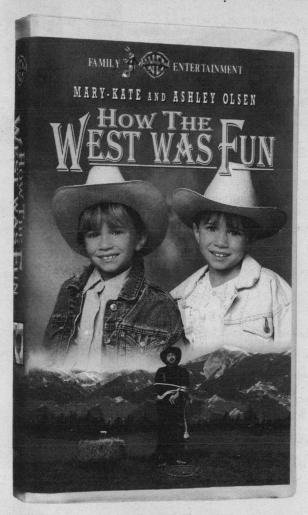

OWN IT ON VIDEO!

SPECIAL OFFER! $5.00 OFF! GET YOUR VERY OWN MARY-KATE & ASHLEY *THE CASE OF THE U.S. SPACE CAMP® MISSION*™ T-SHIRT!

REGULARLY SOLD FOR $17.95, THIS COOL FULL-COLOR, TWO SIDED T-SHIRT HAS THE AWESOME VIDEO/BOOK COVER ART ON THE FRONT AND THE WILL SOLVE ANY CRIME BY DINNER TIME™ LOGO ON THE BACK!

THE CASE OF THE U.S. SPACE CAMP® MISSION™ T-SHIRT COMMEMORATES THE MAKING OF THE NEWEST ADVENTURES EPISODE AND IS HIGH-QUALITY, PRE-SHRUNK, AND 100% COTTON.

- -

Please send me:

_____ Youth large: **The Case of the U.S. Space Camp® Mission**™ Commemorative T-shirt(s)

_____ Adult large: **The Case of the U.S. Space Camp® Mission**™ Commemorative T-shirt(s)

For a total of:

_____ T-shirts x $12.95* each	=_____
California residents please add 8.25% sales tax	=_____
_____ T-shirts X $2.50 each shipping and handling	=_____
Order Total	=_____

* This price reflects $5.00 discount.

Mail order form with check or money order (U.S. funds only) for the total amount to:

Mary-Kate + Ashley's Fun Club™
859 Hollywood Way, Suite 275
Burbank, CA 91505
Please allow 4-6 weeks for delivery

SHIP TO: (PLEASE PRINT)

NAME:_____

ADDRESS:_____

CITY:_____ STATE:_____ ZIP:_____

COUNTRY:_____ PHONE: (_____) _____